All You Need Is Love

A celebration of **love** stories & **love** songs

"If music be the food of love, play on."
— William Shakespeare

Hello! Here's something you may want to know about the story you are about to read. Each one of the short stories in this collection have been inspired by love and music that connects to loving memories. The story as a whole, the names, characters, places, circumstances, experiences, incidents, and even the liberties taken with time and space, were all created or connected in this specific way to tell this story. Any resemblance to actual events, locales, businesses, experiences, or persons, living or dead, is entirely coincidental, personal to the author, or part of the storytelling process. So, in the sprit of storytelling, I hope you find a nice place to sit back, relax, and turn the page!

First published in the United States of America on 2025 by Calelei™ Productions.

If you would like to use any material from this book please contact us at
hello@caleleiproductions.com

ISBN: 978-1-958807-16-3
eISBN: 978-1-958807-17-0

Library of Congress Control Number: 2022921762

ABOUT THIS BOOK:
"All You Need Is Love (A Collection Of I Love Yous)" By Isabel K.T.
First Edition, October 2025 | First Print, October 2025 | English Language

The fonts used in this book were "Bellota" for the cover, the chapter headings, the titles, the stories, & the details, "Open Sans" for the front-matter and technical details, and "Encode Sans SemiExpanded" for all other text. Cover design by Isabel K.T.

Please note that the publisher is not responsible for any other website (or content) other than the publishers'. Visit us anytime:

Calelei™ Productions
www.caleleiproductions.com

We love Trees. Follow our tree planting at caleleiproductions.com/trees

"Two the love of my life - I love you, Always."

Out there, there is a song, that brings to life happy memories and loving thoughts. Perhaps there are many songs that bring back happy memories and loving thoughts. To me love songs evoke the warmth of a loving moment with my dearest, bring back the memories of a moonlit kisses, of starry nights holding hands, or a of a rising sun on a lazy morning, memories of a tender caress, a loving touch, the wish to be in that loving moment at any given time... It is in love songs that I have come to find small time capsules filled with wonder that bring me to those moments at any given time simply by pressing play.

"If music be the food of love, play on."
— William Shakespeare

Within these pages you may find familiar tunes and re-discover in them precious moments, explore with them a novel space of hope and love, or discover new melodies and gentle reminders of the wonders of love, all dancing to their own tune. This collection of short stories is for those who express through song what words alone cannot reach, and for those who reach with song what words best express, within this pages melody and story combine to simply say in every kind of way — I LOVE YOU.

In short, this book is a collection of love stories inspired by love songs. May it bring a little love to your reading.

Volume I. Stories

Can't Take My Eyes Off Of You

"You're just too good to be true, can't take my eyes off of you..." the song plays in her head as she walks along the streets of everywhere. She barely notices her feet are subtly dancing to it's rhythm with each step she takes. Once upon a dream she found herself understanding these lyrics for the first time. In truth, as far as lyrics go, they are rather self explanatory. Two eyes meet, souls recognize each other, the bodies that contain them urge them to stay in that meeting — where it all feels right —

there is warmth, there is hope, a tingling sensation all too ethereal and easily confused with weakness appears to encourage levity in the body, and the inclination to hold with touch springs forth to — if only for a moment— make sure it is all real.

What is there not to understand in that? It is all there, plain and simple, expressed to words & music. *Or is it?*

It all started four weeks ago. She walked into a cafe to get her usual order when their eyes met.

Funnily enough this song was playing in the background. His order came up, she didn't catch his name, just his eyes. He seemed as hesitant as her to let go of the moment as he reached for the cup with what seemed like a latte. Almond milk if she was judging by the density of the milk, and she was. His friend came over with a reminder they were late for their next meeting.

Just then a swarm of giggly teenagers came into the cafe. It seemed like a quick coffee run, she could remember seeing them waiting in line with their tickets for the concert next door. She could faintly make out their conversation, she wasn't particularly interested, her eyes did not want to leave him yet her shorter frame made it easy for their connection to get interrupted and by the time she looked up he was gone.

Love at first sight? If you asked she would simply reply, "I don't know. When I see him again I'll confirm if I believe that." Yet deep in her heart something new had begun to awaken. *Was he too good to be true? Or was he just perfect in the matching ways he could be to her?* Granted she did not believe in perfection, it seemed too man-made a word to warrant the liveliness of nature, but that moment, that moment was indeed perfect. Interruptions and all.

It happened again just a week after that. She was at her favorite bookstore perusing titles in different sections, one for cooking, one for technical design, one for romance... when she pulled out an anthology of Shakespeare's plays and saw those same two eyes looking straight at her. Her heart lightened. *Was it the same person?* All she had was a pair of eyes to go by, and yet she knew — yes, he was. Just then her friend came into the store with exciting news "I have exciting news." That's all she heard her friend say because she tried, ever so unsuccessfully, to catch another glimpse of his eyes. He was gone. She sighed and returned all her attention to her friend who had very exciting news indeed!

Then two weeks ago, she was walking in the park trying to figure out how to solve the missing piece for her current project when a car drove by playing Frankie Vally's version of "Can't take my eyes off of you." She looked up to see a kid with a big sparkly kite coming out of his car window that read "Would You Go To Prom With Me?" She smiled. *How could she not smile at that? What are the odds?* Prom didn't exist where she grew up, and she didn't think she ever missed out on anything, yet every year when she saw the creativity kids came up with just to express a loving overture it reminded her of how wonderful it is to be so fully open to love.

This time it was different, it felt different, the moment she saw that kite, the moment she heard that song, it meant more. The moment brought back flutters to her heart and she slowly started to realize the true value a love song can have. This song wasn't just her reminder of a tender moment with a stranger, it was a celebration of love for someone else, and hopefully it was about to also become a loving memory between two kids. Perhaps there was a reason this song kept finding it's way to her, perhaps all it really was saying was "keep believing."

As far as things go, belief is quite free, and so is hope. *Oh what a little song could do for the heart,* She thought. Before she realized it she had hastened her pace and as she did she discovered a new rhythm filled with possibilities — in them came the answer she was

looking for, finally that "aha"
moment that put the pieces of her
project together: *Music! It needed
the right music!*

A week ago her friends
invited her to a new place called
Rooftop Cinema for a movie night.
She didn't even look at what they
were going to see, she just said yes
and it wasn't until she arrived that
she started second-guessing her
choice. Posters for Jaws and
Twister were the first thing she saw
as she exited the elevator. She
hoped she hand't signed up for

that, but just in case she made her way to the candy counter and got some popcorn. She almost grabbed a bag of fruit jellies to have a little extra sweetness with her just in case it was a scary movie, however, she decided it was going to be ok either way and just took the popcorn. Little did she know the movie they were about to watch was "Ten Things I Hate About You" (Exactly! who can think about this movie without remembering the iconic moment where Heath Ledger hires the marching band to sing

"Can't take my eyes off of you" to Julia Stiles?). She almost dropped her popcorn when she walked into the theater — almost!   Then, as she walked out of the theater at the end of the movie, she saw an area designated for social media posts. There was a background with a series of bleachers. She is barely pondering on the possibility of it all, when a young girl approaches her and asks if she would film her real quick,

          "Hi, would you mind helping me ? I need to do a really quick shot for my boyfriend, he is out of town and I just want to surprise him with a little serenade? Yes?"

Of course she says "Yes," and shortly after that the girl begins to sing the lyrics she now knows by heart: "You're just too good to be true..."

And this week... This week she heard the song every day, every day... when she turned on the radio (yes, she still liked to listen to the radio when she drove), when she walked into a restaurant, when she walked into a store, even when she walked into a hotel lobby — albeit that instance was without lyrics, just scrumptiously played on the piano.

Every single day she had heard that song except for today... She tried not to think about it this morning on the road when it was missing from the radio, she tried not to read into it when she did not hear it as she walked into the bookstore, she tried not too make too much of it when she tried playing it on her Spotify and it froze. She was making up her mind whether or not she should call it in at the local radio station — you know, just to be sure it was out there in the universe where she properly felt it belonged — when she heard it. It was coming from the cafe she had been at four weeks ago. Someone had just opened the door to exit and a whiff of croissants, coffee, and Gloria Gaynor singing "... You'd be like heaven to touch... I want to hold you so much..." came straight at her (or so it seemed to her anyway).

Could it be? She thought,
"Huh..." she walked slowly to the cafe, feet made up, mind uncertain of what she would find, and there he was... the same man! Their eyes met and she held back her breath as her whole body kept breathing in the same direction. He stood up from the table at the corner and walked up to her with a smile on his face.

He reached out his hand to hers and simply said "Hello,"

"Hello," She replied — it seemed only proper really ...

Four weeks ago he was at a caffe, waiting for his usual order when she walked through the door. Their eyes met, the connection became palpable down to the very fiber of his being. *What is this?* He thought. Before he could say anything his friend came back with a reminder that they were late for their next meeting. Then a swarm of jumping teenagers arrived talking about music or something like that and before he knew it her eyes were gone. He tried looking for her over the series of heads that covered her, he even thought he could spot her head in the crowd, to be honest he wasn't sure — could he?

Then three weeks ago he was at a book store, getting a copy of Rilke for his sister, when he saw those eyes again, looking straight at him from the other side of the book stacks. Suddenly a friend of hers came waltzing through with news, he walked around the bookshelf to catch her before she left, yet before he could say anything she was gone.

It was two weeks ago when he decided he needed to find her, he was heading out of the Rooftop Cinema with some friends when he decided to buy a bag of fruit jellies at the concession stand before calling it a night, perhaps it was a hunch or what-not because just then he heard someone singing loudly "I love you baby, and if it's quite alright I need you baby to warm my lonely nights ... " he looked up and there she was, recording this person. He was positive it was her but he couldn't be sure. Either it was her or he needed to find her and this was yet another sign that he should do something about it. And so he did... That is the moment he decided he would go to the cafe where they met every morning until they saw each other again. Little did he know it would take only a week to find her — & thankful he was for it too.

Today, it was simple, the song started to play at the cafe,

this time it was Gloria Gaynor's version, he was humming it to himself when the doorbell rang, he looked up — there she was. The same eyes he had seen. He'd heard it said before that the eyes are the windows to the soul, and he hadn't given it much thought until now. It seemed that from the windows of his soul to the window of her soul there was barely a distance. He stood up and walked up to her.

There was so much he wanted to say, so he decided to start with "Hello," to his delight she smiled and said "Hello," back. He felt his smile widen and it was then he realized he had been smiling since she walked into the shop.

"Would you have coffee with me?" He said, hoping for a yes.

"Sure" she replied.

It must have been late night when the owner of the small cafe came by to see if they needed anything before the kitchen closed. It felt but moments to them.

"Are you closing now? " He asked.

For the past week the owner of the little cafe had seen him at the same corner table looking up at the door every time someone came through it, and now she knew why.

"Just the kitchen," replied the owner, "you can stay for another hour or so if you'd like." The owner then walked towards the door and turned off the OPEN sign to be sure no new customers arrived.

He turned back to her. She was looking up at the moon, so

clearly visible in a crescent shape from the floor-to-ceiling cafe windows. *It's smiling too, she thought.*

"Would you like to stay?" He asked.

"Yes," She replied with a smile.

They picked up their conversation right where they left it and barely realized the owner had started moping the floors as the song came back up on the cafe speakers... "You're just too good to be true… Can't take my eyes off of you…"

Satellite

"When I am far away all you have to do is look up & you will see my 'I Love You' in the stars..."

      His words echo in the wind around her like a soft whisper. She catches them in the gentle breeze as she remembers a night, not too long ago, where he was there beside her. Before he set sail through space unknown and adventure took them on different paths. She remembers the touch of his cheek to her lips, and the tender stream of warm tears her eyes couldn't hold on to meeting his cheek and escaping into her kiss.

She sighs and looks down at the note in her hand. It felt like yesterday, it always felt as fresh as yesterday since then. The crisp summer air hinting at fall, the trees moving gently with the wind knowing change was coming, their spot— one with nature. They were in their spot. Whether the world knew it or not, it was theirs, it didn't matter who knew because they knew. To them nature kept it safe every season for a star-gazing picnic where they could wonder at the marvels of the universe and hold each other close. Today she sat there, in her place, reserving his for him and him alone.

The last time they were together he'd mapped out her favorite constellations so she would be able to remember how to find them. She could hear his laugh as she tried time and again to find the constellations she loved. She somehow ended up mixing one star or another in the diagram, yet somehow still found the shape of the constellation she was looking for.

"Who organized these anyway?" She would say with a laugh, and every time he would join her in the laugh and then point her in the right direction.

"More like this," He would simply say after, always smiling as he guided her fingers across the night sky, tracing the constellation in question.

I wonder how they look now from up there... She thought. It had been four months since he took the shuttle up — the space shuttle that is — and it had been four weekends that she came by herself to their hilltop and traced the constellations replaying in her mind his voice as he explained the map he drew for her.

He showed her how to find the brightest star in the horizon first, and from there she was able to gather her footing and find the rest.

"In that star you will find a loyal constant. You can follow it anywhere in the world, and it will always shine bright for you to find."

"It's part of Cannis Major?" She'd asked looking at the star.

"Yes, and it is always the brightest star in the night sky. It's not like the Northern Star that it is steadily connected to a Pole. This star moves, yet no matter where it goes you can always recognize it by its brightness, and then you can count on that brightness to help you find the way home."

"Pure puppy love!" She'd said, and before he could say anything, she amended "not the fleeting kind that leaves a loving mark with age. The youthful everlasting feeling of true love, the gentle love, and tender love, and timeless love that waits, and shines, and grows, and moves, choosing perpetuity over permanency, moving in a steady flow always giving it's best, knowing love waits for it too."

"I like that kind of puppy love best," He'd said.

"Me too," She'd answered.

Me too, She thought now again. She looked at her phone, it was late, she better get some rest before ballet tomorrow. She never liked this part, staying in her spot made her feel closer to him somehow... She knew he was coming back — it was just that moment of longing, that moment when all she wanted to do was turn around and see him there that made time hold new meaning. She looked up at the stars and sent a kiss to his favorite, closing her eyes for a moment, wishing he would receive it when he looked at it next. She then grabbed her bag and slowly, as slowly as she could possibly move, started descending down the grassy spiral that led into town.

One, two, three, four… she could hear her teacher clapping her hands to the beat of the dance. One, two, three, four… she knew her feet were moving, she knew her hands were floating in the air — her mind however, was dancing in the stars — *if she could only spin so fast that she could float away and reach him then he would be able to be with her and his stars at the same time...* One, two, three, four... & One, two, three, four... & One, two, three, four... the final claps brought her back to the present moment. With one last pirouette she gently laid her right foot behind her steady left as her hands descended to her sides somehow remembering to emulate the delicate movement made by layered gossamer flying on the wake of a summer breeze.

It's early morning and the sun is still as shiny as it was when he went to sleep a couple of hours ago, time moves differently when you are spinning around earth and not on it. He sighs and looks down at his wrist, her red ribbon is still tied neatly where she left it, "— a gentle reminder that home is always just a few taps away," She had said as she wrapped it lovingly on his wrist. He brings his wrist to his nose for a moment, a miniature gesture that takes him home to her smell. The ribbon had held on to her perfume, and for a second he could breath in her warmth and her smiles, and see her right there with him.

As light pours in through the sunny window it touches the ribbon making the blue undertones of the cherry-red pop, and for a second he remembers the sun *is* another star just shining in it's own way — sunny. That's why he calls this space, 'the Sunny Window,' it's what she would call it too if she could be up there with him. He smiles at the realization that even miles apart they are laughing at inside jokes. *Context is everything,* she would say, and she was right. Most people around them heard one thing, or saw one thing, when in reality — to them it was an entirely different world.

It had happened from the very beginning, the smallest things would take on new meaning — a shared meaning. Buying a tomato at a grocery store, meant smiling at an inside joke. Staring at the moon at night, meant remembering a conversation by a pool of reflective water and a bushy tree cradling the night between it's leaves. Looking up at the sky meant a whispered "I Love You," tendrils of sunlight meant a loving kiss, every part of the day — well, that meant adventure and possibility — And the stars, the stars had taken on a life of their own, a life as loving messengers to kisses and as the bright light in dreams that would guide the way home to each other. Yes, she had turned his world upside down, and as it turned out, he had done the same for her. He could hear her laughing, "Two upside downs means one shared right side up!" And it was...

The stars where shining particularly bright tonight. It wasn't the weekend yet all she wanted to do was run to the hill and sit on their spot. Her agenda was open to the date, his birthday was coming up soon and she wanted to do something special for him. Perhaps if she flashed an "I Love You" in morse code he would get her message... *It's probably too far away for him to see it. Sigh... How do you get a message to outer space?* They had their wall... they always had their wall... but it was not the same, she wasn't sure he was getting any of her messages. She'd promised to write to him every day, and she had, she just wished her messages were loud enough for her to be sure they had reached him. *Fireworks!* She thought. Perhaps fireworks can be seen from the ISS... A quick search lets her know that although they may, perhaps, under very particular circumstances, be seen from afar… it is not the most feasible way to send him an "I Love You." Besides, the amount of fireworks needed for this to maybe-perhaps work was not within her budget.

Her budget was small — practically none existent — yet her wishes were big, all *she had to do was get creative*, she'd told herself. She looks at the note on her desk and then out her window, the sky is so clear she can see some of the stars at a distance. She looks down at the note again, his handwriting saying "I Love You" in every explanation, in every detailed breadcrumb that guided her to find their favorite stars. *Look Up, I am always saying 'I love you,'* He'd said, and he was right. She could see his 'I Love You' every time she looked at the stars. *One day I'll find a way to write on the stars for you so you too can always know my love is with you wherever you go...*

The peanut butter on his hand floats away... He got

distracted, the ribbon on his wrist got stuck on the ISS kitchen table tape as he prepared himself a peanut butter sandwich. *Peanut Butter 'Taco,'* He thought, as there was no actual bread on board. Tortillas however, many! He secretly loved this fact, it only made him feel closer to home and to her. As he grabs the jar of Jif from floating away, he thinks about the many kinds of tacos he's going to make for her as soon as he gets back...

One... two... three... One... two... three... & pivot, & pivot, soubresaut, soubresaut, assemblé, pas de chat, pas de chat, pirouette, & pirouette, & pirouette, arabesque croisseé... With every step she could feel bright warmth at the tips of her toes, with every note a brighter and brighter space surrounding her... Suddenly she sees stars all around her, the more she dances, the more they shine, when her hands fall to her sides to end her piece she turns to look on at the space around her, shinning brightly are stars painting a beautiful constellation with the words 'I love you' visibly traced in the connecting space between each star. She looks around, Is this what I danced? Did I do this? She ponders... As she looks back behind her she wakes up...

I know what to do! She thinks. She closes the physics text book she fell asleep over, grabs her ballet bag and dashes out of her room, only to return a few minutes later to brush her teeth, jump in the shower, and properly get ready for the day ahead.

Finally! She thinks, as she reaches the top of the hill. It is still early morning, the stars are still shining faintly in the early morning sky. She looks down at his note and then at her open notebook. There is now a carefully drawn-out map on it. All she needed was a few tools and calculations, and if her hypothesis worked, he would be seeing a bright shining constellation coming from Earth.

She looks at the field below and then looks up at the trees around her, searching for a good tree branch to start. After a few quick tests, she takes out a series of small mirrors and golf pegs from her bag and gets to work.

Once the mirrors are all safely pasted on the pegs, and the pegs are all safely placed on the ground, she goes up the tree with a smaller bag. There she takes out a bigger mirror and angles it towards the smaller mirrors safely layered on the ground, she then flashes a flashlight towards the bigger mirror until she reaches the right angles and the light from the flashlight lights up the light in the big mirror and the light in the big mirror lights up the light in all the smaller mirrors on the ground. It takes a while but she finds the right flow.

After a please & thank you to the tree & a few creative maneuvers on her part, it is finished. She wiggles her way down the tree and looks at her message. If it works, she'll know when he gets back. *Happy Birthday my love,* She thinks. She sends a kiss to their favorite star and hurries off, down the hill, racing to her classroom.

He floats around the space station, going from one section to the next, he just passed his sunny window, and is craving a view of earth, perhaps, he thinks, perhaps, he can see something that brings him closer to her. The internet had been spotty lately, nothing out of sorts, they were simply flying too high up for proper wifi, still... her messages were always a source of comfort and all he needed was a little glimpse, a touch of hope, that felt like home.

He looks at the red ribbon on his wrist, he was so glad she'd given it to him that day, little did he know how much it would come to help. "It's just a point to focus on, as you spin around," She'd said, "if we are going to spin around then is best to have one, plus it's comforting! In ballet, when you find your spotting point, you can pirouette to your heart's content without loosing your balance or getting dizzy when you 'land' ... so I hope this brings you a bit of that comfort while you spin in your own way up there."

He'd laughed. She always makes him laugh. She hadn't realized it but the best spot turned out to be memories. They were the best memories to keep with him while he was far away — the best company.

It's late, she should have been there earlier, now she'll only have an hour to gaze at the stars.

One hour... she sighs as she sets her bag to one side... it is never enough anyway, might as well make the most of now... She looks down at her work. A few snowflakes have started to fall, far less than yesterday's — easy fix. She takes out a string of small yellow lightbulbs and places them around the pegs. Not too much, just enough to make sure the mirror is surrounded by warm light that can melt the snow. Plus, this way adds an extra layer of brightness to the whole message, just in case.

Once she is done she sits down on her spot, takes out her phone, and quickly kisses his picture before she opens the app that monitors the light display. She makes sure everything is running smoothly and puts her phone away to gaze at the stars and dream uninterrupted. She lays down her blanket and starts finding her favorite constellations with ease... Oh will he be surprised by the time he comes back!

She wakes up, she is still on her spot, she must have dozed off as she thought of all the things they were going to do when he came back. She looks at the time, it's almost 2am. Good thing it had been a warm night, she had barely noticed the light flutter of snow coming at her. She looks up at their favorite star, and sends it a kiss. *I'll see you tomorrow, She thinks.*

It's almost Christmas. Almost perhaps is a strong word, yet it is almost Christmas to her — three more weeks to go! She sits down at her spot, and checks her light system. Everything seems to be working just fine, it is time for her to just relax and enjoy the moment. She used to dread the time apart until she realized, instead of missing him she could use every moment she missed him in to write him a note, and then by the time he came home he would know just how missed he was and just how loved he is, it also gave her something to do with all that missing — *Definitely a win-win, She'd thought.*

She takes out her note pad and pen, and is about to write him a message when something falls on her lap. She gasps. It's her ribbon. *Wait, is it? It certainly looks like her ribbon...* She looks left and right... no one in sight. *Just a sugar rush,* She thinks. She holds the ribbon in her hand and gives it a gentle squeeze, if only it had been hers...

"I believe you have something that is mine," He says.

She looks up, amazed, startled, excited, grateful, a million emotions coursing through her veins and she just smiles and says,

"Really? Come and get it then!"

He sits down next to her, on his

spot, his smile matches hers.

"Hello," He says.

She grabs the collar of his jacket

and pulls him in for a soft and

tender kiss.

"Welcome home," She says

as she lays her head on his

shoulder, he finds her hand and

intertwines his fingers with hers as

he lays his head atop hers.

They look on at the stars

together. 'I Love You' shines brightly

above them, as Cannis Major lends itself for a most beautiful note of everlasting Puppy Love.

(Four-ever in Bloom)

A Never-ending Story

"Since the day I met you I realized a very important truth, love heals, and in that healing, love grows anew. It is an ever flowing cycle of life in constant bloom. Much like the flowers I love to grow, in each I see now a token of your love and a reminder of all the beauty there is to enjoy when you get to enjoy together. With a little bit of hope and a little bit of love, inspiration can take us exactly where we need to be. I hope in this you can see expressed what your flowers have always meant to me — love in bloom — and the certainty of tomorrow filled with it, for you live in my heart always."

He puts down the note. She holds out her hand. He takes it.

"Close Your Eyes," She says, and she gently walks him along the path before them.

"Do you remember the first time you bought me flowers? You were coming back from rehearsals, your guitar on toe, and I was crying because — "

"— Your flowers had just died. "

"I knew it was coming, it's part of their natural cycle, I knew, I just wasn't ready for it."

"I know sweetheart,"
Without opening his eyes, he pulls her hand to his lips and gives her a gentle kiss.

"You held my hand, and we talked, and the next day I woke up to a bag of seeds and the sweetest note that read 'Plant new seeds,'"
She smiled.

"I remembered what you'd told me, you'd said, 'Plant some more & they'll bloom, they always do,' & You were right , of course, I just hadn't thought of it in that way."

"I remember."

They keep walking.

"May I open my eyes now?"

"Not quite there yet,"

"Alright. May I know what we are doing?"

"You'll see." She gives him a reassuring kiss on the cheek.

"Ok, then."

"Then, when I got back home the next day —"

"I didn't mean then then," He says.

"Oh, I know, it just fits, because *then* I had a bag full of sunflower seeds waiting for me on the front door, with a lovely note in a melody that reminded me 'Plant New Seeds, They'll Bloom' and I did and they did. Then you surprised me with seeds and music the week after that, and the week after that, and you have been surprising me with inspiration every moment since."

"I see what you did there."

"Just you wait!"

"May I open my eyes now?"

"Almost."

He can hear the faint creeks of a door's hinges as they move onto a different patch of land. "Now?"

"Wait For it..."

The grass beneath his feet is a welcome swishing mushy alternative to the hardened floor of stone he'd just stepped out of, mushy and curious for now something was definitely afoot. She stopped and gently turned him around.

"Now?"

"Now."

All around him in a crescent shape he could see flowers layered and arranged to the sound of the song he'd written for her. There, before him were the flowers he gave her, growing in full bloom, surrounding him in a hug of color and sweet perfume. The faint buzzing of a bumblebee added the perfect soundtrack to the painted picture. At a glance, he could see a year of memories, looking closely he could hear the notes in each flower singing their song in an ever lasting cycle of life and love and bloom.

"Can You Hear Them?"

"When did you do this?"

"I started the first day you brought the sunflower seeds and I've been working on it since."

"Darling, I don't know what to say..."

"You my dear are the most beautiful melody I have ever heard, & I am grateful everyday to have you in it."

"I love you."

"I know."

He kisses her. She kisses him back and starts to hum the tune they love.

He holds her close, hips swaying to the melody, they hum together in a dance as bumble bees and butterflies join in the song.

"There's a story too you know?" She says.

"Oh?"

"Would you like to hear it?"

"Absolutely," He answers, placing a loose strand of her hair behind her ear and kissing her cheek.

She tells him the story as they dance:

There once was a girl who loved flowers, & her garden was precious to her. There once was a boy who loved music, & melodies were precious to him. One day the boy saw her at work in her garden & asked what her favorite flower was.

"That is a difficult question to answer. I love them all. Hmm, my favorite may be the bright ones that look like their hair is in the wind, I just planted these today. If you ever want to bring me flowers," She said "I'd rather have the seeds, that way I can plant them & watch them bloom & grow over & over & over again." She showed him her latest work, "These are about to bloom, it is a very exciting time."

A few days passed when the boy happened upon her at her garden again, this time there were tears strolling down her eyes.

"What's wrong?" He asked.

"They bloomed & they withered, I knew it would happen but, I wasn't prepared to watch." She said.
He held his hand to her and with the other found the seed the flowers had left behind. Then he gently placed it in her hand and closed her hand a top of it.

"Plant the seed, & they will bloom again! Right?" He smiled. The boy had a smile that could light up the world, & in that moment, he filled hers with love, joy, & possibility. She held on to his hand & together they planted that seed.

He was right, that was all she needed to do. All she could do, and it was enough. That single moment warmed her heart so much she'd gotten to the garden and decided to do something special with those seeds, just for him.

She took out her notebook, her pens, and her measuring tools, and got to work. Little did she know what would follow. As the seasons came she would find a new flower to grow, a new seed to plant, and a new bloom.

Time passed & every day the boy would bring seeds for her to plant. As the garden grew, so did their love blossom. One day he looked up & she was waiting for him before he reached the door. She kissed him tenderly, held out her hand for his, & gently told him "Close your eyes." She then walked him to the center of the garden & whispered "It is safe to look now," & He did.

Before him, flowers in full bloom, their favorite colors, all arranged as a love note singing their favorite songs.

"I wanted you to see a little bit of what your love brought into my life" She said, " Color & music & joy everlasting. I will love you forever, & so will this garden bloom always."

"That story sounds very familiar" He says grinning wide.

"Doesn't it?" She answers matching his grin.

"And is that how the story ends?"

"No sweetheart, it's always how the story begins! Plant new seeds remember?"

"Always."

"Always."

Have I Told You Lately

That I Love You ...

A little gift... well... a little gift can go a long way, by mere intention alone... just wait & see ...

*   A little boy walks along with a note in his hand, the image of a cherry-red heart-shaped balloon is on it. A gust of wind comes by and whisks it out of his hands, we see him go after the card.

*   A little girl walks along with a little note in her hand.

*   She goes into a shop that sells balloons.

*   She comes out of the shop with a big cherry-red heart-shaped balloon in her hand and a smile on her face.

* As she walks out onto the street, the wind comes and blows the balloon away.

* She follows the balloon into the city.

* The balloon flies over the city.

* A couple holding hands sees the balloon, a little girl walking her dog sees the balloon, people at a construction site see the balloon, a man inside a cab with a briefcase sees the balloon, an artist on the street sees the balloon, a cotton candy maker with a cotton candy stand sees the balloon... an ice cream truck driver sees the balloon...

* The balloon stops on a tree in the
  park, right by a bluebird's nest.

* The little girl arrives to see it
  stuck on a branch.

* She tells the balloon to wait and
  goes to get help.

* A wind comes by and frees the
  balloon.

* The little girl comes back and the
  balloon is gone.

* The balloon lands on a puddle in
  the park.

* A photographer is looking for
  something to capture.

* The photographer sees the balloon through the camera and snaps a picture.

* A mother passes by taking her baby for a stroll around the park.

* The photographer cleans the balloon and gives it to the mother with the stroller.

* The mother holds the balloon as her baby smiles at the balloon.

* The little girl arrives to see the balloon being walked away.

* She sighs.

* She walks over to a bench nearby and sits there.

* A little boy arrives, and sits next
  to her.

* She takes out a card with the
  balloon illustration on it, a little
  sad that she has no balloon.

* The little boy smiles, and he takes
  out a scrunchie, and a note with
  a hear-shaped balloon that
  matches the one on her note.

* The little girl laughs. The little boy
  laughs. They laugh together.

* Suddenly the wind blows and the
  balloon flies into the little boy's
  hand just as a note falls onto her
  lap.

* The little girl smiles and gives him
her card with the balloon
illustration on it.

* They hold hands and walk
around the park and into the city
together.

* As they walk they pass the
stroller parked by a bench, the
baby and mom are looking up,
watching as two loving bluebirds
ready their nest. They pass a
photographer who is looking at
his camera while he paints a
heart-shaped balloon on a
canvas.

* They pass an ice cream truck
with heart shaped ice-pop's and
greet a couple passing by holding

hands and enjoying a pair of pops from the truck. They pass a little girl walking her dog and a small balloon.

* They walk into the city and they pass a sculptor inside a building sculpting a bunch of balloons floating together into the sky. They walk by a graffiti artist painting a balloon on a sidewalk, while a businessman in the building in front is proposing a balloon business. They pass by a cotton candy stand with heart shaped cotton candy, ... as they keep walking a hot-air balloon passes over them leaving balloons all over the city ...

* They walk hand in hand, smiling,
  & they find many a balloon along
  the way of their road everlasting.

Dream a little Dream of Me

The sun goes down on the horizon, He sighs, another day on the road. He puts his headphones in and presses play on an all too familiar tune, a special song between them… "Stars shining bright above you… sweet kisses say and whisper 'i love you' …" He starts to hum along "while you're asleep and sweet as can be, dream a little dream of me…"

It's been, well, too long. If He had to number time He would know the exact figure, yet he tried to avoid looking at that minuscule detail — it wouldn't make anything better anyway. He pulls up his hoodie and rests his head along the window of his train seat. *Almost there*, He thinks, *We are almost there...* This all started when the project he was finalizing took a longer turn. Little did He know what longer meant, little did She know what longer meant. In the end it didn't matter, they found a way for longer to mean something beautiful.

He looked down at his phone, the playlist She created for

him was the only thing visible.
She'd hid in little voice notes
between songs. She wasn't very
comfortable with her voice, yet She
wanted him to hear how much She
loved him from her firsthand & mini
voice notes at the end of each song
seemed like a good way to do so.
He was grateful for that. He missed
her voice. He knew what She would
say:
  *"Not as much as I miss
yours!"* He smiled at the thought.

He would then probably say, "Ok, just for tonight" and then She'd argue,

"No no, just until we see each other again, then you can miss mine more — although I don't know how as I will be surely talking to you about EVERYTHING I didn't get a chance to."

He would simply smile and say "Hmmm, perhaps, however, I still want that right."

And She'd say "Fine, you drive a hard bargain but I will agree to it. I get to miss you more until I *see you again, and you get to miss me more after."*

He yawned, this was the best part of day, only a few minutes and he'd be dreaming of her in his arms. He grabbed his jacket and bunched it up together before placing it under his head as he curled up in his sit.

It was dawn, not her favorite time of day by far. She had just woken up from a perfectly glorious dream with him in it. Sigh, only a few more days and She'd get to wake up in his arms again. She'd get to kiss him good morning and they'd get two smile over pancakes. She was so grateful He was just as cheesy as her. She turned on her phone, the playlist He made for her was playing. She could see He was playing hers. She smiled.

This was the closest to sleeping in the same bed. Music had become a shared comforter that kept the nights warm and the mornings breezy. Day by day it covered their embrace as each melody played the road on their way back home to each other. The song was in it's last chorus "Sweet kisses come and find you, sweet kisses leave all worries behind you... while you are sleep and sweet as can be, dream a little dream of me..." She sent him a kiss with a wish it would leave all worries behind him and the added wish for sweet dreams. *We are almost there sweetheart, We are almost there,* She thought. She picked out a song for him and started it so He would know She was awake, then sent him a quick text "Sweet dreams Angel, I love you."

It had been a long time, She could scarcely believe it, at times it felt like it would be forever, other times it felt like the time apart had barely happened. Either way one thing remained the same, there is no way she would not hide in the suitcase next time. She got ready, grabbed her tablet and a change of clothes, placed them quickly in her bag, prepared a quick strawberry-mango-banana smoothie (with a dash cinnamon and 1/2 a cup of orange juice) and dashed out the door.

She was almost done with the day, it was 7pm but She was almost done with the day, when she realized the playlist was coming to an end. She quickly grabbed her phone and closed the door to her office to start a new recording of songs and voice-notes for when his tomorrow began.

"Good night Sweetheart, have a fantastic day!" She says into the phone as she tags the next song, " Stars shining bright above you… " As the song eases into the background She kisses his picture and then get her attention back to work. *Almost there*, She thought, *Almost there…*

He woke up to the sound of a notification chiming in, a quick look and a wide smile later, He presses play on her latest creation and lets their songs lull him to sleep for a few more minutes. The train came to it's next stop, and the gentle pull of the brakes reminded him there was a reason for this stop on his itinerary. He yawns himself awake and keeps the music going letting it subtly score his morning.

Two more hours to go and He'd be back on the train and in her arms. In dreams at least, and that — for now— was everything. He passed by a market, She would love it. He knew it, so he took out his phone and snapped a picture of items he could hear her voice in. One booth had beautiful rocking flower vases. He knew He couldn't leave without one. I mean he could, but he most definitely wouldn't.

He'd find the perfect flower for it when He got home. With a smile on his face, He gets on the train, carefully places the vase between his sweater and scarf in his brown duffle bag, and sits down just before the doors close. He sighs, another day, another adventure.

He takes out his phone, presses play to the playlist he is half-way through listening and rests his head against the window. He wakes up to the touch of an icy window. He had been in a beautiful dream, the stark contrast between the warmth of the sky in it and the icy window He was sleeping on, woke him up. It was a little past midnight. He pulls his beanie out of his pocket and puts in on quickly. Then takes his phone out of the other pocket and after quickly unraveling a slight knot on his earphones, presses play again on his playlist. He looks at their picture for a moment before he rests a warmer head on the windowsill. "Stars shining bright above you..."

"... while you're asleep and sweet as can be, dream a little dream of me…" She wakes up to the sound of his voice "Good morning sweetheart!" She fell asleep with her earphones in. It was almost perfect. Almost. The sun was streaming through the window, and music was streaming his love. *We may not be there yet, She thought, yet Almost is starting to have a beautiful flavor to it too. She thinks.* She sighs and looks at the phone, it is time to wake up. She has a long day ahead.

Her latest draft took a lot more to complete than She'd

intended. As She got her copies bound, She heard a familiar tune coming from the FedEx speakers and smiled. It was moments like these that made the playlist all the more special. It was always a melodic way to tell each-other about their day. She quickly Shazams the tune and adds it to the playlist along with a voice note "I did it! I finished the presentation and am getting it bound. Look what came out on the speakers. (Shazam Link Inserted Here) BTW I Love You More!"

She smiled, She could practically hear him counter it with

"Not a chance!"

"Just for tonight?" She'd reply, and there was a 70% chance he'd say, *"Ok."* The other 30% was always filled with a fun and cheeky alternative that made her laugh and want to kiss him, so either way it was a win - win in her book.

She missed him, plain and simple. There was a gentle tap on her shoulder. She looked around, the lady behind her was pointing towards the desk, her presentation was ready. She quickly thanks the lady and walks over to pick up her booklet, all the while secretly imagining him next to her holding back a laugh. She holds back her own and shakes her head as she exits the store, slightly embarrassed at the things that didn't happen in public.

His coffee had gone cold, he only noticed when he tried to take a zip from it. He'd gotten distracted by the road when rows and rows of winter trees lined up to say 'hello'. He takes out his phone, snaps a quick picture of the trees, and turns it into the official picture of his new playlist. The first song on the playlist comes quickly 'Fleetwood Mac's Everywhere,' He smiles. Who knew little moments could be so loving? This adventure had certainly brought to the forefront the monumental value of little things in day-to-day life. Not that he needed this adventure to know it, yet it was a welcome reminder of how much he loved sharing all those little things with her.

He snuggles into his hoodie and zips his coffee, it may be cold, but it is still flavorful. While he debates on whether or not to get a new cup or just a bit more warm water for it, a new playlist comes through. He can't contain the laugh. He hadn't posted his, but hers, hers was a beautiful copy, it was a different tree, in a different part of the world, yet it was the same tree saying 'hello.' He opens the newly arrived playlist, at the very top in what seems to him to be shining letters is 'Fleetwood Mac's

Everywhere.' There may be distance between them but they were never truly apart. He loves the playlist and the song and presses play, the smile on his face widening with each note.

She wakes up, her smile ongoing, he'd sent his playlist in perfect time, just before she fell asleep, and she couldn't help but notice her draft playlist for today matched almost verbatim what he had sent her. It was a lovely thought to sleep with. She had quickly sent him a 'copiche' text next to the images of her draft and his playlist side by side. His respond had her smiling even more, little did she know that he was creating the same playlist she had sent him the day before. Trees and all, there was clearly no space love could not reach.

The sun is out, it's soft tendrils reach her face and in a moment she is elsewhere remembering his touch, gentle, tender, kind. Bright refreshing warmth, that was the easiest way to describe it. She presses send on her latest playlist and quickly adds a good morning voice note for him to know she is awake.

As she walks in the morning sun, she starts to realize she is dancing. Not an obvious dance, perhaps only the curious passerby would notice, yet a gentle pep accompanies every step with levity and rhythm. *Funny,* she thinks, *The one time I am not listening to music, and yet I am still dancing.* Her phone chimes in with a reminder of her "to-day" list (a far easier way to tackling her to-do list) "croissants, cafe, emails, pt, Zumba, presents, prototype…" that's all it said. She looks up from her phone to find a sycamore tree right across the street from her. She laughs, quickly snaps a pic and sends it to him alongside a short voice note "… birds singing in the sycamore tree… dream a little dream of me…"

She then goes home, answers emails, makes croissants, enjoys one with a nice cup of coffee, places a few on a pink paper box and runs off to Zumba.

He receives a notification, it's a message a lovely sycamore tree and a voice note. He puts his earphones back on to listen and smiles. He sends her a kissy chippy gif and presses play on the latest playlist. He is enjoying the most delightful Sunday when suddenly woken up to "Bye Bye Bye." Confused and a little startled he looks at his playlist. Something's off. Just then a message comes in.

"Sorry! Zumba playlist mishap. I Love YOU!" Embarrassed

emoji face and kissy face follow. He holds back a laugh.

He texts back, "You had me worried for a second there."

"What? Goodbye is not in my vocabulary to you — ever." She answers.

"Ditto." He replies.

She sends him a new link, "Is it Too Late Now To Say Sorry?"

He laughs, and sends one in response, "Nothings Gonna Change My Love For You… "

She answers with "You are Just Too Good To Be True," and then adds "Dream A little Dream of Me…" with a short text "Sweet Dreams Angel, I've got you!"

He smiles and sends a response, "Nothings Gonna Stop Us Now" followed by "Everlasting Love."

She loved his response. She knew why he sent it, *"Love is everything and goes beyond nothing."* *To infinity & beyond* she thought with a smile.

He pulls out his scarf from his duffle bag and a tin can falls out while he does it. He picks it up. It used to be filled with Mliamr cookies, their favorite. Of course, they majority lasted very little, the last one he made it count taking little pieces off a day at a time. He opens the can. The last crumb is there. He looks at his watch, only hours to go before he would be home. He enjoys the last bit and falls asleep dreaming of more.

After Zumba she comes home, jumps in the shower, and as

her to-day list suggests, she works on her latest invention prototype. Once she reaches a roadblock she moves on to wrapping their Christmas presents and writing up their cards. She then looks at her watch a and decides to make some Mliamar cookies just in case he comes home while she sleeps.

The cookies are in the oven. She sets the timer and goes to get ready for bed. With the last of the presents wrapped and most of the cards done, the only ones pending are those he will add something to himself when he gets home, she looks at the house. The Christmas decorations are up and everything seems ready, yet something is missing. *Obviously him…* She looks at the wall in front of her, it looks bare. She goes for her painting set, gets her paint overalls on and starts to work. She adds a new song to her playlist for him, sends it his way, and presses play on his playlist to her as she paints.

   This is it, the last stop, He thinks. *After this, Home.* He crosses the last item on his list. The project is finished and everything is ready and set up for his own project in the new year. Something he wants to pitch to her and her alone once the holidays are over.

He gets off the train, his friends are there to greet him. They go on a hike and talk about his project. On the way back he sees a bouquet of beautiful colorful flowers and without a second thought gets them for her.

All aboard he thinks, as he takes on the last train stop home...

It's late night, early morning even, when he arrives home. He quietly drops his duffle bag by the entrance bench and heads to the kitchen to find a vase to place the flowers in. He wants them to be a surprise for her when she wakes up. Little did he know what was waiting for him when he arrives.

He goes out to the living room with the bouquet safely set on a clear glass vase and he stops in his tracks. On the wall in front of him are the same flowers, painted across from left to right. He can't help but smile.

He then looks at the table, a plate full of Mliamar cookies is waiting for him at the center. He places the vase with flowers on the table right by the cookies and grabs a single flower from the arrangement.

He then takes his shoes off and tip-toes up the stairs.

She feels soft petals on her cheek and smiles, the only thing sweeter is knowing the hand that is on the other end of that loving caress. Without a second thought She pulls him in for a tender kiss and a warm embrace.

"Welcome Home Sweetheart." She whispers to him as She kisses each corner of his lips.

"Honey, I'm Home," He laughs between kisses,

"I think I noticed," She says with a mid-kiss smile.

"Yeah, I think you've noticed too." He answers matching her smile.

After a moment of kiss-full bliss,
She curls up to the nook in his
neck.

He remembers something.
"Hang on!"

"No! Why do you want to
leave me?!" She holds onto him.

"I have a surprise for you—"

She pulls him back into bed,
"Nope, I love it, I know I do, right
now I just want to be with you."

"Ok then," He curls into bed
with her.

She snuggles next to him
and starts singing to him ever so

softly "Stars shining bright above you, sweet kisses say and whisper 'I Love You,'

He sings softly back to her "...while You're asleep and sweet as can be, dream a little dream of me..." He kisses her cheek and holds her in his harms. "Good night sweetheart."

She snuggles in closer and kisses his chin, "I love you."

All You Need Is Love.

"Two the love of my life – I Love YOU, Always."

All You Need Is Love

A pocket-sized collection of "I **Love** You" in the form of short-stories inspired by **love** and **love** songs.

Calelei Productions

www.caleleiproductions.com

* 9 7 8 1 9 5 8 8 0 7 1 6 3 *